Anonymous

AF137029

Laws Relative to Quarantine and to the Public Health of the City of New-York

SALZWASSER
VERLAG

Anonymous

Laws Relative to Quarantine and to the Public Health of the City of New-York

Reprint of the original, first published in 1858.

1st Edition 2023 | ISBN: 978-3-37515-250-5

Verlag (Publisher): Salzwasser Verlag GmbH, Zeilweg 44, 60439 Frankfurt, Deutschland
Vertretungsberechtigt (Authorized to represent): E. Roepke, Zeilweg 44, 60439 Frankfurt, Deutschland
Druck (Print): Books on Demand GmbH, In de Tarpen 42, 22848 Norderstedt, Deutschland

LAWS

RELATIVE TO

QUARANTINE

AND TO THE

PUBLIC HEALTH

OF THE

City of New-York.

———•———

1858.

LAWS
RELATIVE TO
QUARANTINE
AND TO THE
PUBLIC HEALTH
OF THE CITY OF NEW-YORK.

——————◆——————

PART 1st, CHAPTER XIV.,
OF THE
REVISED STATUTES,
AS AMENDED AND MODIFIED BY THE SUBSEQUENT ACTS OF THE LEGISLATURE.

——————◆——————

TITLE I.

OF THE OFFICERS OF THE PUBLIC HEALTH IN THE CITY OF NEW-YORK.

§ 1. The legislative powers heretofore vested, by *Board of Health.* any existing law of this State, in the Board of Health of the city of New York, other than as the same are hereinafter modified or altered, shall be vested in the Mayor and Common Council of the said city of New York. (1850, *ch.* 275, § 1.)

§ 2. The said Mayor and Common Council, when *Ib.* acting in relation to the public health of said city, or in the execution of the said powers, or those hereinafter conferred, shall be known as the Board of Health of the city of New York, of which ten

Quorum. members shall be necessary to constitute a quorum.
President. The Mayor shall be the President of such Board, and shall have power at any time to convene the same. (*Same ch.* § 2.)

Sessions. § 3. The sessions of the Common Council, when acting as a Board of Health, shall be with closed doors, except when otherwise ordered by said Board. (*Same ch.* § 3.)

Commissioners of Health. § 4. The President of the Board of Aldermen, the President of the Board of Assistant Aldermen, the Health Officer, the Resident Physician, the Health Commissioner, and City Inspector, shall be the Commissioners of Health. (*Same ch.* § 4.)

To advise the Board. § 5. It shall be the duty of the Mayor and the Commissioners of Health to render their advice to the Board of Health, and to the City Inspector of said city, in regard to all matters connected with the public health thereof. (*Same ch.* § 5.)

Health Officer. § 6. The Health Officer shall perform all the duties hereinafter specified, and such other duties as the Board of Health, or the Mayor and the Commissioners of Health, shall lawfully require. (*Same ch.* § 6.)

Assistant Health Officer. § 7. The Health Officer may appoint an assistant, for whose conduct he shall be responsible, and who may perform all the duties required of the Health Officer. Such assistant shall, before entering on the duties of his office, take the oath prescribed in the Constitution of this State. (*Same ch. § 7.*)

§ 8. The Resident Physician shall visit all sick persons reported to the Board, or to the Mayor, and the Commissioners of Health, and shall perform such other professional duties as the Board of Health shall enjoin. (*Same ch. § 8.*)

Resident Physician.

§ 9. The Health Commissioner, under the direction of the Board of Health, shall assist the Resident Physician in the discharge of his official duties. *Same ch. § 9.*)

Health Commissioner.

§ 10. (Sec. 8.) He shall also receive all moneys appropriated to the use of the Marine Hospital, and shall pay all demands against the Hospital that shall be approved by a majority of the Commissioners of Health, and, before he shall enter on the duties of his office, shall execute a bond in the penal sum of twenty thousand dollars, conditioned for the faithful performance of his trust, and with such sureties as the Mayor or Recorder of the city shall approve. The bond shall be given to the people of this State, and be filed by the officer taking it, in the office of the clerk of the city and county. (*As amended* 1840, *ch.* 19.)

Ib. to give Bonds.

§ 11. (Sec. 9.) He shall render to the Board of Health a monthly account of his receipts and disbursements on account of the Marine Hospital, and shall deposit the balance that shall appear to

To Account and Deposit.

be in his hands in such bank in the city of New-York as the Board shall designate, to the credit of the Commissioners of Health.

Moneys, how drawn.

§ 12. (Sec. 10.) The moneys so deposited shall not be drawn out, except on the check of the Health Commissioner countersigned by the President of the Board of Health.*

Commissioners to meet.

§ 13. In the discharge of their duties, the Mayor and the Commissioners of Health shall meet daily at the office of the Board of Health, during such part of the year and at such hours of the day as the said Board shall designate. (1850, *ch.* 275, § 10.)

Salaries of Resident Physician and Health Commissioner.

§ 14. The Resident Physician shall receive an annual salary of twelve hundred and fifty dollars, to be paid by the Corporation of said city, and the Health Commissioner an annual salary of three thousand and five hundred dollars, in lieu of fees and percentage, which shall be paid by the Commissioners of Emigration; and after the expiration of the term of office of the present Health Commissioner and Resident Physician, the said officers

---

* The transfer of the control of the Marine Hospital to the Commissioners of Emigration, by chapter 483 of the laws of 1847, has rendered the provisions of the original sections 8, 9, and 10, of this title, in many respects inoperative. But they have not been specifically repealed, and it is possible that cases may arise under existing laws where moneys may be received and disbursed as directed in these sections. They are therefore inserted entire.

shall hereafter be appointed by the Mayor of the city of New-York, by and with the advice and consent of the Board of Aldermen of said city.* (*Same ch.* § 12).

§ 15. The Board of Health may, from time to time, appoint so many visiting, hospital and consulting physicians, as they may deem necessary, designate their duties, and fix their compensation. (*Same ch.* § 12.)

Consulting Physicians may be appointed.

§ 16. The Mayor, by and with the advice and consent of the Board of Aldermen, may appoint an Inspector of Vessels, who shall, under the direction of the Mayor and the Commissioners of Health, or of the Board of Health, perform the duties required of him in this act, and shall be entitled to receive the following fees:

Inspector of Vessels.

For each cargo inspected by him, under such direction, three dollars.

Fees.

For each vessel cleansed and purified by him, under the like direction, five dollars.

Which fees shall be paid by the owner or consignee of the cargo inspected, or vessel cleansed and purified. (*Same ch.* § 13.)

---

* Modified by section 7 of chapter 523, laws of 1851, so as to make the salary of the Health Commissioner payable out of the city treasury, and be fixed by the city authorities.

§ 17. It shall be the duty of such Inspector, after he shall have performed any service required cf him, to make an immediate report of his proceedings, and their result, to the Board of Health, or to the Mayor and the Commissioners of Health. (*Same ch. § 14.*)

TITLE II.

OF QUARANTINE, AND REGULATIONS IN THE NATURE OF QUARANTINE AT THE PORT OF NEW-YORK.

ARTICLE FIRST.

Of the Place of Quarantine, and Vessels and Persons subject to Quarantine.

Anchorage Ground. § 1. The anchorage ground for vessels at Quarantine shall be near the place where the Marine Hospital now is, and shall be designated by buoys to be anchored under the direction of the Health Officer; and every vessel subject to quarantine shall, immediately on her arrival, anchor within them, and there remain, with all persons arriving on her, subject to the examinations and regulations imposed by law. (1856, *ch.* 147, § 1.)

Quarantine of Vessels. § 2. Vessels arriving at the port of New-York shall be subject to quarantine as fcllows: 1st. All vessels from any place where pestilential, contagious or infectious disease existed at the time of their departure, or which shall have arrived at any such place, and proceeded thence to New-York, or on board of which, during the voyage, any case of such disease shall have occurred, arriving between the first day of April and the first day of November, shall remain at Quarantine for at least thirty days after their arrival, and at least twenty days after their cargo shall have been discharged, and shall perform such further quarantine as the Mayor and Commissioners of Health may prescribe, unless the Health Officer, with the approval of the Mayor or Commissioners of Health, shall sooner grant a permit for said vessel or cargo, or both, to proceed. 2d. All vessels from any place (including islands) in Asia, Africa, or the Mediterranean, or from any of the West Indies, Bahama, Bermuda or Western Islands, or from any place in America, in the ordinary passage from which they pass south of Cape Henlopen, and all vessels on board of which, during the voyage, or while at the port of their departure, any person shall have been sick, arriving between the first day of April and the first day of November, and all vessels from a foreign port, not embraced in the first subdivision of this section, shall, on their arrival at the Quarantine Ground, be subject to visitation by the Health Officer, but shall not be detained beyond the time requisite for due examination and observation, unless they shall have had on board during the voyage some case of infectious, contagious or pestilential disease, in which case they shall be subject to such quarantine and regulations as the

Health Officer and the Mayor, or Commissioners of Health may prescribe. 3d. All vessels embraced in the foregoing provisions, which are navigated by steam, shall be subject only to such length of quarantine and regulations as the Health Officer shall enjoin, unless they shall have had on board during the voyage some case of infectious, contagious, or pestilential disease, in which case they shall be subject to such quarantine as the Health Officer and the Mayor or Commissioners of Health shall prescribe. (*Same ch. § 2*).

Ib. § 3. All vessels and persons remaining at Quarantine on the first day of November, shall, thereafter be subject to such quarantine and restrictions as vessels and persons arriving on and after that day. (*Same ch. § 3.*)

When vessels at wharves of the city may be removed to Quarantine Ground. § 4. The Board of Health, or the Mayor and Commissioners of Health of the city of New-York, or the Board of Health of Brooklyn, or the Health Officer of the Port of New-York, whenever in their or his judgment the public health shall require, may order any vessels at the wharves of the city, or in their vicinity, to the Quarantine ground or some other place of safety, and may require all persons, articles or things introduced into the city from such vessel, to be seized, returned on board thereof, or removed to the Quarantine or other place of safety. If the master, owner, or consignee of the vessel cannot be found, or shall neglect or refuse to obey the order of removal, the said Board of Health or Mayor and Commissioners of Health, or Health Officer, shall have power to employ such assistance as may be necessary to effect such removal, at the expense of such master, owner or consignee; and such vessel or person shall not return to the city without a written permission of the said Board of Health, or Mayor and Commissioners of Health, or Health Officer. Whenever any person shall have been employed as above provided, to remove any vessel, or to remove any article or thing introduced into the city from such vessel, and shall, in pursuance of such employment, effect such removal, he shall have a lien on such vessel, her tackle, apparel and furniture, for his services and expenses in effecting such removal. (1857, *ch.* 412, § 1.)

§ 5. Whenever the said Health Officer, in the performance of the duties, and in the execution of the powers imposed and conferred upon him by law, or by any regulation or ordinance made in pursuance of any statute of this State, shall order or direct the master, owner, or consignee of any vessel under quarantine to remove such vessel from her anchorage, or to do any act or thing, or comply with any regulation relative to said vessel, or to any person or thing on board thereof, or which shall have been brought to said port therein, and said master, owner or consignee shall neglect or refuse to comply with such order or direction, the said Health Officer shall have power to

Special powers of the Health Officer.

Liens on Vessels. employ such persons and assistance as may be necessary to carry out and enforce such order or direction, and the persons so employed shall have a lien on such vessel, her tackle, apparel and furniture, for their services and expenses. (*Same ch.* § 2.)

Liens defined. § 6. The liens specified in the preceding Sections may be enforced in the same manner as other liens are enforced, by warrant of attachment, in the mode prescribed in Title Eight of Chapter Eight of the third part of the Revised Statutes, all the provisions of which Title shall apply to the services and expenses specified in this Act; and the person or persons so rendering such services, and incurring such expenses, shall be deemed creditors of such vessel, and of her master, owner or consignee, respectively; or such person or persons may have and maintain an action against the master, owner or consignee respectively; or such person or persons may have and maintain an action against the master, owner, or consignee, or either of them, of such vessel, to recover the value of such services and expenses. (*Same ch.* § 3.)

Vessels bound to Eastern ports. § 7. If any vessel arriving at the Quarantine Ground, subject to quarantine, shall be bound to some port east of the city of New-York, the Health Officer, after having duly visited and examined her, may permit her to pass on her voyage through the Sound; but no such vessel shall be brought to anchor off the city, nor shall any of her crew or passengers land in, or hold any communication with, the city, or any person therefrom. (1856, *ch.* 147, § 5.)

§ 8. Every vessel having had, during the voyage, a case of pestilential, infectious, or contagious disease, and every vessel from a foreign port having passengers, and not hereinbefore declared subject to quarantine, shall, on her arrival at the Quarantine Ground, be subject to visitation by the Health Officer, but shall not be detained beyond the time requisite for due examination, unless she shall have had on board, during the voyage, some case of infectious, contagious, or pestilential disease, in which case she shall be subject to such quarantine as the Health Officer, and the Mayor, and the Commissioners of Health may prescribe; and it shall be the duty of the Health Officer, whenever he thinks it necessary for the preservation of the public health, to cause the persons on board any vessel to be vaccinated. (1850, *ch.* 275, § 7.) *Infected Vessels.*

§ 9. The master of any vessel released from Quarantine, and arriving at the city of New-York shall, within twenty-four hours after such release, deliver the permit of the Health Officer at the office of the Mayor. (1856, *ch.* 147, § 6.) *Permit to be delivered at Mayor's Office.*

§ 10. Nothing in this act contained shall prevent any vessel, arriving at Quarantine, from again going to sea before breaking bulk. (*Same ch.* § 7.) *Restriction*

ARTICLE SECOND.

Of the Duties of Pilots in relation to Vessels subject to Quarantine.

Duty of Pilots. § 11. It shall be the duty of each branch and deputy pilot belonging to the port, to use his utmost endeavors to hail every vessel he shall discover entering the port, and to interrogate the master of such vessel in reference to all matters necessary to enable such pilot to determine whether, according to the provisions of the preceding sections, such vessel is subject to quarantine or examination by the Health Officer. (*Same ch.* § 8.)

Notice to Master of Vessel. § 12. If, from the answers obtained from such inquiries, it shall appear that such vessel is subject to quarantine or examination by the Health Officer according to the preceding provisions, the pilot shall immediately give notice to the master of the vessel, that he, his vessel, his cargo, crew and passengers, are subject to such examination, and that he must proceed and anchor said vessel at the Quarantine anchorage, there to await the further directions of the Health Officer. (*Same ch.* § 9.)

Duty of Pilots in charge of vessels. § 13. It shall be the duty of every pilot, who shall conduct into port a vessel subject to quarantine or examination by the Health Officer:

1st. To bring such vessel to anchor within the buoys marking the Quarantine anchorage.

2d. To prevent any vessel or boat from coming alongside of the vessel under his charge, and to prevent anything on board from being thrown into any other vessel or boat.

3d. To present to the master of the vessel a printed copy of this title, when such copy shall have been delivered to him for that purpose.

4th. To take care that no violations of this title be committed by any person, and to report such as shall be committed, as soon as may be, to the Health Officer. (*Same ch.* § 11.)

ARTICLE THIRD.

Regulations concerning the Treatment, Conduct, and Duties of Vessels, Articles and Persons under Quarantine.

§ 14. It shall be the duty of the Health Officer to board every vessel subject to quarantine or visitation by him, immediately on her arrival, between sunrise and sunset; to inquire as to the health of all persons on board, and the condition of the vessel and cargo, by inspection of the bill of health, manifest, log-book, or otherwise; to examine on oath as many and such persons on board as he may judge expedient, to enable him to determine the period of quarantine and the

[margin: Health Officer to board Vessels.]

regulations to which such vessel shall be made subject, and to report the facts and his conclusions, and especially to report the number of persons sick, and the nature of the disease with which they are afflicted, to the Mayor or Commissioners of Health in writing. (*Same ch. § 11.*)

Residence of Health Officer.

§ 15. It shall be the duty of the Health Officer to reside within the Quarantine inclosure, and he shall have power:

To remove dangerous Vessels.

1. To remove from the quarantine anchorage ground any vessel he may deem dangerous to the public health, to any place south of the Quarantine buoys and inside of Sandy Hook.

Cargo and passengers to be landed.

2. To cause any vessel under quarantine, when he shall judge it necessary for the purification of the vessel or her cargo, passengers, or crew, or either of them, to discharge or land the same at the Quarantine Ground or some other place out of the city.

Ventilation and cleaning of Vessels.

3. To cause any such vessel or her cargo, bedding, and the clothing of persons on board, to be ventilated, cleansed and purified, in such manner and during such time as he shall direct; and, if he shall judge it necessary, to prevent infection or

Cargo may be destroyed.

contagion, to destroy any portion of such bedding or clothing, and, with the authority of the Mayor or Commissioners of Health, any portion of such cargo which he may deem incapable of purification.

4. To prohibit and prevent all persons, arriving in vessels subject to quarantine, from leaving Quarantine, or removing their baggage or goods therefrom, until fifteen days after the last case of pestilential, contagious, or infectious disease shall have occurred on board, and ten days after her arrival at Quarantine, unless sooner discharged by him, with the consent of the Mayor and the Commissioners of Health.

Prohibition as to leaving Quarantine.

5. To permit the cargo of any vessel under quarantine, or any portion thereof, when he shall judge the same free from infection and contagion, to be conveyed to the city of New-York or elsewhere; such permission, however, to be inoperative without the written approval of the Mayor or Commissioners of Health.

Permit to proceed to N. Y.

6. To cause all persons under quarantine to be vaccinated, when he deems it necessary, for the preservation of the public health.

Vaccination.

7. To administer oaths and take affidavits in all examinations prescribed by this act, and in relation to any alleged violation of quarantine law or regulation; such oaths to have the like validity and effect as oaths administered by a commissioner of deeds. (*Same ch.* § 12).

To administer oaths.

§ 16. The Health Officer, or the Physician of the Marine Hospital may direct, in writing, any constable or other citizen, to pursue and apprehend

Persons eloping from Marine Hospital may be arrested. any person, not discharged, who shall elope from Quarantine, or who shall violate any quarantine law or regulation, or who shall obstruct the Health Officer, or the Physician of the Marine Hospital, in the performance of their duty, and to deliver him to said officer or officers, to be detained at Quarantine until discharged by said officer or officers; but such confinement shall in no case exceed ten days. It shall be the duty of the constable, or other citizen so directed, to obey such directions; and every such person so eloping or violating the quarantine laws and regulations, or obstructing the Health Officer, shall be considered guilty of a misdemeanor, punishable with or by fine and imprisonment. (*Same ch.* § 13).

Care of the sick. § 17. Every sick person sent to the Marine Hospital, by the Health Officer, shall be there kept and attended to with all necessary and proper care, and no such person shall leave the Hospital until the Health Officer shall grant a dischage in writing. (*Same ch.* § 14.)

Indigent emigrants. § 18. The Commissioners of Emigration shall remove from the Marine Hospital and take charge of all indigent emigrants, whose quarantine has expired, and who shall have sufficiently recovered from the diseases with which they were admitted, on the notification in writing of the Health Officer, that such removal will not, with ordinary care, endanger the safety of the individual, or the health of the community. (*Same ch.* § 15.)

§ 19. The Health Officer, the Board of Health, or the Mayor and Commissioners of Health may, if in their opinion it will not be dangerous to the public health, permit the cargo of any vessel under quarantine, or any portion thereof, to be shipped for exportation by sea, or transportation up the North or East River; and if the vessel receiving the same shall approach nearer than two hundred yards to the wharves of the city, said cargo may be seized and sold by the Mayor and Commissioners of Health for the use and benefit of the Marine Hospital. (*Same ch.* § 16.)

When cargo may be shipped for sea.

§ 20. Every vessel during her quarantine shall be designated by colors, to be fixed in a conspicuous part of her main shrouds. (*Same ch.* § 17.)

Designation by colors.

§ 21. No vessel or boat shall pass through the range of vessels lying at Quarantine, or land at the Quarantine Grounds or wharves, without the permission of the Health Officer. (*Same ch.* § 18.)

Permit required to pass through range of vessels.

§ 22. No lighter shall be employed to load or unload vessels at Quarantine without permission of the Health Officer, and subject to such restrictions and regulations as he shall impose. (*Same ch.* § 19.)

Lighters not to be employed without permit.

§ 23. All passengers being on board of vessels, under quarantine, shall be provided for by the master of the vessel in which they shall have arrived; and if the master shall omit or refuse to

Passengers under Quarantine how provided for.

provide for them, or they shall have been sent on shore by the Health Officer, they shall be maintained by the Commissioners of Emigration at the expense of such vessel, her owners, consignees, and each and every one of them; and the Health Officer shall not permit such vessel to leave Quarantine until such expense shall have been repaid or secured; and the said Commissioners shall have an action against such vessel, her owners and consignees, and each and every one of them for such expenses, which shall be a lien on such vessel, and may be enforced as other liens on vessels are enforced by said Commissioners. (*Same ch. § 20.*)

Persons charged with offence may be confined on shore. § 24. The Health Officer, upon the application of the master of any vessel under quarantine, may confine, in any suitable place on shore, any person on board of such vessel charged with having committed an offense punishable by the laws of this State or of the United States, and who cannot be secured on board of such vessel; and such confinement may continue during the quarantine of such person; or until he shall be proceeded against in due course of law; and the expenses thereof shall be charged and collected as in the last preceding section. (*Same ch. § 21.*)

Appeal, to whom to be made. § 25. Any person aggrieved by any decision, order or direction of the Health Officer, may appeal therefrom to the Mayor and Commissioners of Health of the city of New-York, who shall constitute a Board of Appeal; the said Board shall have power to affirm, reverse or modify the decision, order or direction appealed from, and the decision of said Board thereon shall be final. (*Same ch.* § 22.)

§ 26. An appeal to the Board of Appeal must be made by serving upon the Health Officer a written notice of such appeal within twelve hours (Sundays excepted) after the appellant receives notice of the order, decision or direction complained of. Within twelve hours after the Health Officer receives such notice, (Sundays excepted,) he shall make a return in writing, including the facts on which his order, decision or direction was founded, to the Mayor, who shall immediately call a meeting of the Board of Appeal, and shall be president of said Board; and said appeal shall be heard and decided within twenty-four hours thereafter (Sundays excepted;) and until such decision is made, the order, decision or direction complained of, except it refer to the detention of a vessel, her cargo or passengers at quarantine, shall be suspended. (*Same ch.* § 23.)

How made

Health Officer's return of facts.

Decision.

ARTICLE FOURTH.

Of the regulation of intercourse with infected Places.

§ 27. The Mayor of the City of New-York may issue his proclamation, declaring any place where

Proclamation by Mayor.

there shall be reason to believe a pestilential, contagious or infectious disease exists, or may exist, to be an infected place within the meaning of the health laws of this State. (*Same ch.* § 25.)

Publication of notice.

§ 28. Such proclamation shall fix the period when it shall cease to have effect; but such period, if they shall judge the public health requires it, may from time to time be extended by the Board of Health of said city ; and notice of the same shall be published in five or more of the newspapers of the city. (*Same ch.* § 25.)

Effect of proclamation.

§ 29. After such proclamation shall have been issued, all vessels arriving in the port of New-York, from such infected place, shall be subject to the same quarantine laws and regulations as the vessels embraced in the first subdivision of the second section of this act, and shall, together with their officers, crews, passengers and cargoes, be subject to all the provisions, regulations and penalties of this act, in relation to vessels subject to quarantine; but such quarantine shall not extend beyond the period when such proclamation shall cease to have effect, as provided by the last preceding section. (*Same ch.* § 26.)

Intercourse with infected places, by whom regulated.

§ 30. The Board of Health may, in their discretion, prohibit or regulate the internal intercourse, by land or water, between the city of New-York, and such infected place; and may direct that all persons, who shall come into the city of New-

York contrary to their prohibitions and regulations, shall be apprehended and conveyed to the vessel or place from whence they last came; or, if sick, they shall be conveyed to the Marine Hospital, or such other place as the Board of Health shall direct. (*Same ch.* § 27.)

ARTICLE FIFTH.

Penalties for violating the Provisions of this Title.

§ 31. Every master of a vessel subject to quarantine, or visitation by the Health Officer, arriving in the port of New-York, who shall refuse or neglect either : Penalties by masters of vessels.

1. To proceed with and anchor his vessel at the place assigned for quarantine, at the time of his arrival ;

2. To submit his vessel, cargo and passengers, to the examination of the Health Officer, and to furnish all necessary information to enable that officer to determine to what length of quarantine and other regulations they ought respectively to be subject; or,

3. To remain with his vessel at Quarantine during the period assigned for her quarantine, and while at Quarantine to comply with the directions and regulations prescribed by law, and with such as any of the officers of health, by

virtue of the authority given to them by law, shall prescribe in relation to his vessel, his cargo, himself, his passengers, or crew, shall be guilty of a misdemeanor, and be punished by a fine not exceeding two thousand dollars, or by imprisonment not exceeding twelve months, or by both such fine and imprisonment. (*Same ch.* § 28.)

§ 32. Every master of a vessel, hailed by a pilot, who shall either :

1. Give false information to such pilot, relative to the condition of his vessel, crew or passengers, or the health of the place or places from whence he came, or refuse to give such information as shall be lawfully required;

2. Or land any person from his vessel, or permit any person, except a pilot, to come on board of his vessel, or unlade or tranship any portion of his cargo before his vessel shall have been visited and examined by the Health Officer ;

3. Or shall approach with his vessel nearer the city of New-York than the place of quarantine, to which he may be directed, shall be guilty of the like offence, and be subject to the like punishment; and any person who shall land from any vessel, or unlade or tranship any portion of her cargo under like circumstances, shall be guilty of the like offence, and be subject to the like punishment. (*Same ch.* § 29).

§ 33. Any person who shall violate any provision of this act, or neglect or refuse to comply with the directions and regulations which any of the officers of health may prescribe, shall be guilty of the like offence, and be subject for each offence to the like punishment. (*Same ch.* § 30.)

By other persons.

§ 34. Every person who shall oppose or obstruct the Health Officer in performing the duties required of him by law, and every person who shall go on board of, or have any communication, intercourse, or dealing with, any vessel under quarantine, or with any of her crew or passengers, without the permission of the Health Officer, or who shall, without such permission, invade the quarantine grounds or anchorage, shall be guilty of a misdemeanor, and shall be punished by a fine of not less than one hundred, nor more than five hundred dollars, or by imprisonment, not less than three nor more than six months in the Penitentiary; and such offender shall be detained at Quarantine so long as the Health Officer shall direct, not exceeding twenty days. In case such person shall be taken sick of any infectious, contagious, or pestilential disease, during such twenty days, he shall be detained for such further time, at the Marine Hospital, as the Health Officer shall direct. (1856, *ch.* 147, § 31, 32, and 1857, *ch.* 412, § 4.)

Punishment for obstructing the Health Officer.

Punishment for holding communication with vessel, &c., without permit.

Offender may be detained at Quarantine

§ 35. Exclusive jurisdiction of the offences specified in the preceding section is hereby given to

Jurisdiction of offences.

the Courts of General and Special Sessions of the Peace of the City of New-York; and it shall be the duty of the District Attorney of the City and County of New-York to prosecute all persons guilty of such offences in preference to any indictment then in his office; and it shall be the duty of either of said Courts to hear and try the offence against this act in preference to all other cases pending before it; and whenever any person shall be convicted on a trial for such offence, the Court shall forthwith proceed to pronounce judgment upon him, according to the terms prescribed in this act. (1857, *ch.* 412, § 5.)

Special duty of District Attorney and Courts.

Speedy trial, and no suspension of sentence.

Penalty for other acts.

§ 36. Every person who shall violate the provisions of this act, by refusing or neglecting to obey or comply with any order, prohibition, or regulation made by the Board of Health, in the exercise of the powers herein conferred, shall be guilty of a misdemeanor, punishable by fine and imprisonment, in the discretion of the court by which the offender shall be tried. (1856, *ch.* 147 § 33.)

Jurisdiction of offences.

§ 37. The Courts of General and Special Sessions of the Peace of the city and county of New-York shall have exclusive jurisdiction of all offences against the provisions of this act; and it shall be the duty of the District Attorney of the city and county of New-York to prosecute all persons guilty of such offences without delay. (*Same ch.* § 34.)

Rule 1

§ 38. Section six of article one of title two of

chapter two hundred and seventy-five of the laws of eighteen hundred and fifty, and sections fifteen and twenty-two of article three of title two of the same chapter of the laws of eighteen hundred and fifty, and section thirty-five of article five of the same law, and section seventeen of chapter five of title five, of part first of the Revised Statutes, together with all laws inconsistent herewith, are hereby repealed. (*Same ch.* § 37.)

TITLE III.

INTERNAL REGULATIONS FOR THE PRESERVATION OF THE PUBLIC HEALTH OF THE CITY OF NEW-YORK.*

ARTICLE FIRST.

Of certain Duties and Powers of the City Inspector, the Board of Health, and the Mayor and Commissioners of Health.

§ 1. The City Inspector of the City of New-York shall have power— City Inspector.

1. To appoint, by and with the advice and consent of the Board of Aldermen of said city, from time to time, all and so many Health Wardens and other officers as the Common Council or the Board of Health shall direct, to carry into effect the provisions of this title, and the rules and regulations Health Wardens.

---

* Title 3 of Chapter 275 of 1850 substituted for title 3 R. S.

of the Board of Health, the laws and ordinances of the Common Council of said city, and the laws of this State relating to the public health. Such Health Wardens and Officers shall be subject to the supervision and control of the City Inspector.

Their duties. 2. To authorize such officers, at such times as he shall think fit, to enter into and examine in the day-time all buildings, lots, and places of every description within the city, and to ascertain and report to the Mayor and the Commissioners of Health the condition thereof, so far as the public health may be affected thereby.

Duty of City Inspector on complaint. 3. It shall be the duty of the City Inspector, on complaint being made to him, or whenever he shall deem any business, trade, or profession, carried on by any person or persons in the city of New-York, detrimental to the public health, to notify such person or persons to show cause, before the Board of Health, at a time and place to be specified in such notice, why the same should not be discontinued or removed, which notice shall be a notice of not less three days, (except in case of epidemic or pestilence, the Board of Health may, by general order, direct a shorter time, not less than twenty-four hours.) and may be served by leaving the same at the place of business or residence of the parties to be affected thereby. Cause may be shown by affidavit, and the order of the Board of Health shall be final and conclusive thereon.

4. The said City Inspector to give all such direc- Cleansing
tions, and adopt all such measures for cleansing and puri-
and purifying all such buildings, lots and other ings, &c.
places, and to do or cause to be done everything,
in relation thereto, which, in the opinion of the
Mayor and the Commissioners of Health of the
city, shall be deemed necessary. Every person
who shall disobey any order of the City Inspector,
or of the Board of Health, which shall have been
personally served upon them, to abate or remove
any nuisance in the manner and at the time de-
scribed in such order, shall, on complaint of the
City Inspector, or of the person serving such
order, before the Mayor or any Police Justice of
said city be liable to arrest, and summary punishment by fine, not exceeding one thousand dollars,
or imprisonment not exceeding one year, or by
both such fine and imprisonment.

5. To adopt such prompt measures, to prevent Further
the spreading of any contagious, infectious, or duties.
pestilential disease, as shall be directed by the
Mayor and the Commissioners of Health, when it
shall appear to the Mayor and Commissioners of
Health that any person within the city is afflicted
with any disease of that character.

§ 2. The Mayor, Aldermen and Commonalty of By-laws.
the city of New-York shall have full power and
authority to make and pass all such by-laws and
ordinances as they shall from time to time think
necessary and proper, for the preservation of the

public health of said city, and also for the abatement and removal of all and every nuisance in said city, and for compelling the proprietors or owners of the lot or lots, upon which the same may be, to abate and remove the same.

Nuisances. § 3. It shall be lawful for the said Mayor, Aldermen and Commonalty, in all cases where they may deem it necessary for the more speedy execution of said by-laws or ordinances, or any of them, to cause any such nuisance or nuisances to be abated or removed at their own expense, and they are hereby authorized to levy and collect the sum or sums so expended, with lawful interest and all reasonable costs and expenses attending such proceedings, by distress and sale of the goods and chattels of the proprietors or owners of the lots and premises, from which such nuisance or nuisances shall have been abated or removed, or to recover the amount of every such expense, by action in any court of record, from such owner or owners respectively, on whose account the same shall have been expended, their respective heirs, executors, or administrators; in all which actions they shall, also, recover lawful interest upon the amount of said expense from the time of payment thereof, with full costs of suit.

Expenses of removing. § 4. That the amount of every such expense, which the said Mayor, Aldermen and Commonalty shall incur or pay, as aforesaid, on account of the owner or owners of such lots or premises, for the abatement or removal of any such nuisance or nuisances, shall be a real incumbrance upon the lots and premises from or upon which nuisance or nuisances shall be abated or removed, and shall bear lawful interest until paid, and that the same may be recovered or the payment thereof, with costs, enforced in like manner, as if the said lots and premises were mortgaged to the said Mayor, Aldermen and Commonalty for the payment thereof.

§ 5. It shall be the duty of the Board of Health— Duties of Board of Health.

1. To cause any avenue, street, alley, or other passage whatever, to be fenced up or otherwise inclosed, if they shall think the public safety requires it, and to adopt suitable measures for preventing all persons from going to any part of the city so inclosed.

2. To forbid and prevent all communication with the house or family infected with any contagious, infectious, or pestilential disease, except by means of physicians, nurses, or messengers, to carry the necessary advice, medicines, and provisions to the afflicted.

3. To adopt such measures, for preventing all communication between any part of the city infected with a disease of a pestilential, infectious, or contagious character, and all other parts of the city, as shall be prompt and effectual.

4. To procure suitable places for the reception of persons sick of any pestilential, infectious, or contagious disease, and, in all cases where sick persons cannot otherwise be provided for, to procure for them proper medical and other attendance and provision.

5. To publish, from time to time, all such regulations as they shall have made, in such manner as to secure early and full publicity thereto.

6. To issue warrants to any constable or police officer in said city, to apprehend and to remove such person or persons as cannot otherwise be subjected to the regulations by them adopted; and, whenever it shall be necessary so to do, to issue their warrant to the Sheriff of the city and county of New-York, to bring to their aid the power of the county; all which warrants shall be forthwith executed by the officers to whom the same shall be directed, who shall possess the like powers, and be subject to the like duties, in the execution thereof, as if the same had been duly issued out of any court of record in this State.

When cargo may be removed or destroyed. § 6. The Board of Health, or the Mayor and the Commissioners of Health, when they shall judge it necessary, may cause any cargo, or part of cargo, or any matter or thing within the city, that may be putrid or otherwise dangerous to the public health, to be destroyed or removed; such removal, when ordered, shall be to the Quarantine Ground, or such other place as the Board of Health shall direct; such removal or destruction shall be made at the expense of the owner or owners of the property so removed or destroyed, and the same may be recovered from such owner or owners, in an action at law, by the Mayor, Aldermen, and Commonalty of said city.

§ 7. The Board of Health may send to the Marine Hospital or such other place as the Board of Health may direct, all aliens and other persons in the city, not residents thereof, who shall be sick of any infectious, pestilential, or contagious disease. The expense of the support of such aliens or other persons shall be defrayed by the Corporation of the city of New York, unless such aliens or other persons shall be entitled to be supported by the Commissioners of Emigration. *Non-resident sick to be sent to Hospital*

§ 8. The Board of Health shall have power to take possession of, and occupy, for temporary hospitals, any building or buildings in the said city, during the prevalence of an epidemic, if, in their judgment, the same may be required, and shall pay for private property so taken, a just compensation for the same. *Hospitals, temporary.*

§ 9. It shall be the duty of the Mayor and the Commissioners of Health, from time to time, to communicate to the Board of Health all reports that shall be made to them, or either of them, under *Mayor and Commissioners of Health to report.*

the provisions of this law; and it shall be the further duty of the Mayor and the Commissioners of Health, and of each of them, so to communicate all information in their power that may the better enable the Board of Health to preserve the health of the city.

ARTICLE SECOND.

OF THE DUTIES OF PHYSICIANS AND OTHER PERSONS.

Duties of
Physicians

§ 10. It shall be the duty of each and every practicing physician in the city of New-York;

1. Whenever required by the Board of Health, or the Mayor, and the Commissioners of Health of said city, to report to the City Inspector of said city, at such times, and in such forms as said Board may prescribe, the number of persons attacked with any pestilential, contagious, or infectious disease attended by such physician for the twenty-four hours next preceding, and the number of persons, attended by such physician, who shall have died in said city during the twenty-four hours next preceding such report, of any such pestilential, contagious, or infectious disease.

2. To report in writing to the City Inspector, the Board of Health, or to the Mayor and the Commissioners of Health, every patient he shall have laboring under any pestilential, contagious, or infec-

tious disease, and within twenty-four hours after he shall ascertain or suspect the nature of the disease.

3. To report to the City Inspector, when required by the Board of Health, the death of any of his patients who shall have died of disease, within twenty-four hours thereafter, and to state in such report the specific name and type of such disease.

§ 11. Every person keeping a boarding or lodging-house, in the city of New-York, shall, whenever required by the Mayor and the Commissioners of Health, report in writing to the City Inspector, the Board of Health, or the Mayor and the Commissioners of Health, the name of every person who shall be sick in his house, within twelve hours after each case of sickness shall have occurred. *Boarding-house keepers.*

§ 12. Every master, owner or consignee of a vessel, lying at a wharf, or in a harbor of the city of New-York, shall make a like report, and within the same period, of the name of every sick person on board such vessel, and no person shall be removed therefrom without a written permit for that purpose from the Board of Health, or the Mayor, or one of the Commissioners of Health. *Masters and owners of vessels.*

§ 13. It shall be the duty of each Commissioner of Health, and of each visiting, hospital and consulting physician, to make an immediate report to *Physicians violating act to be reported.*

the Board of Health, of the name of every practicing physician by whom he shall have reason to believe the provisions of the tenth section of this title have been violated; and, if such physician shall neglect or refuse to perform his duty, the Board shall suspend him from his office, and he shall, moreover, be liable to such further penalty as the said Board shall prescribe.

ARTICLE THIRD.

PROHIBITIONS AND PENALTIES.

Packing salted provisions may be prohibited. § 14. The Board of Health shall have power to prohibit, at such times and for such period and periods of time as they shall see cause, the packing or repacking of any salted provisions in any and all parts of the city.

Ib. § 15. No salted or pickled beef, pork or fish, (except smoked beef and fish,) shall be deposited in such parts of the city, during the period or periods of time so prohibited by the Board of Health under the last preceding section.

Exception. § 16. The last preceding section shall not be construed to prevent retail grocers, or other small dealers, from keeping on hand, for the use of their customers, small quantities, not exceding five barrels, of each kind of provisions therein mentioned, if the provisions so kept be sound and in good order.

§ 17. All salted or pickled provisions, and all hides, skins, and cotton, that may be deposited in those parts of the city wherein the Board of Health shall prohibit the packing or re-packing of salted provisions, at the time or times when such prohibition may be made, shall be reported forthwith, by the owner or person having charge thereof, to the office of the City Inspector, that the same may be examined, and, if necessary, destroyed or removed. *Prohibited articles when deposited to be reported.*

§ 18. If such articles, when ordered to be removed by the City Inspector, shall not be forthwith removed by the owner or person having charge thereof, the City Inspector shall cause them to be removed to some safe place, there to remain at the risk of the owner. *To be removed.*

§ 19. The expense of the removal, and subsequent storage of such articles, shall be borne by the owner or person having charge thereof, when removed, and, if paid in the first instance by the City Inspector, may be recovered by the City Inspector, in an action against such owner or bailee; or, if payment of such expenses be refused by the owner or bailee, the City Inspector may cause such articles to be sold, and shall account for the proceeds, deducting such expenses and the cost of sale. *Expense thereof to be borne by owner.*

§ 20. Nothing contained in this article shall be construed to extend to provisions exposed for sale *Exception.*

by butchers in the public markets, or kept by the heads of families for family use.

Penalties § 21. Every person who shall refuse or neglect to obey the directions of this article, or of the Board of Health, or City Inspector, pursuant thereto, in relation to the provisions and other articles above mentioned, shall be considered guilty of a misdemeanor, and, on conviction, shall be subject to fine or imprisonment, or both, at the discretion of the Court. Such fine shall not exceed one thousand dollars, and such imprisonment shall not exceed two years.

Rags, hides and s' ins, prohibition § 22. No rags, hides, or skins, arriving in the port of New-York, shall be deposited in any part of the city, within which the Board of Health shall have prohibited the packing or re-packing of salted provisions, and all such articles, brought into the city contrary to the above provision, may be seized and sold by the Mayor and the Commissioners of Health for the use of the Marine Hospital.

Exception. § 23. The Board of Health, or the Mayor and Commissioners of Health, may, however, permit sound hides and skins to be brought into any part of the city, in small quantities, and for the purpose of immediate manufacture, but not otherwise.

Damaged § 24. It shall be the duty of the master and owner of every vessel that shall have brought cotton in-to the city, between the first day of May and the first day of November, in any year, and of the owner and consignee of such cotton, if, upon examina-tion, it shall appear damaged, or otherwise unsound, to make an immediate report thereof to the Mayor and the Commissioners of Health. <small>cotton to be report-ed.</small>

§ 25. Every master, or owner, or consignee, re-fusing or neglecting to perform the duties so enjoin-ed, shall, for each offence, forfeit to the Commis-sioners of Health the sum of five hundred dollars. <small>Penalty for neglect to report</small>

§ 26. Every person who shall violate any regu-lation, order, or direction of the City Inspector, or of the Board of Health, made or given in the exer-cise of any powers vested in them by any section of this title, shall be considered guilty of a misde-meanor, and, on conviction thereof, be subject to fine or imprisonment, or both, at the discretion of the Court. Such fine shall not exceed one thous-and dollars, and such imprisonment shall not ex-ceed two years. <small>Penalty for violating any section of this Ti-tle.</small>

§ 27. Every practicing physician, who shall re-fuse or neglect to perform the duties enjoined on him by the tenth section of this title, shall be con-sidered guilty of a misdemeanor; and shall also forfeit for each offence the sum of two hundred and fifty dollars, to be sued for and recovered by the Board of Health. <small>Physicians liable to punish-ment.</small>

Penalties.

§ 28. Every keeper of a boarding or lodging-house, and every master, owner or consignee of a vessel, who shall refuse or neglect to obey the orders and directions of the Mayor and the Commissioners of Health, as provided in the eleventh and twelfth sections of this Title, shall be considered guilty of a misdemeanor; and, on conviction, shall be fined for each offence in a sum not exceeding two hundred and fifty dollars, or be imprisoned for a term not exceeding six months.

ARTICLE FOURTH.

GENERAL PROVISIONS.

Power to extend provisions of this act.

§ 29. Whenever it shall appear to the Board of Health that any of the provisions of this Act, limited in their operations to a certain period of the year, ought to be extended, the Mayor of the city shall issue his proclamation, extending such provisions to such time as shall be determined on by said Board, and such provisions shall thereupon be extended accordingly, and with the like effect as if the periods mentioned in the proclamation had been herein enacted.

Mayor may revoke proclamation.

§ 30. If it shall appear to the Board of Health, while such proclamation is still in force, that the necessity of extending the period therein name l has ceased, the Mayor, by a new proclamation, declaring that fact, shall revoke the proclamation issued pursuant to the preceding section, which shall then cease to have effect.

§ 31. All fines, forfeitures, and penalties impos- Fines and ed in this act, or under the powers delegated there- penalties, in, shall be paid to the Health Commissioners, to how collected. and for the use of the city of New-York, and such as are recoverable by suit shall be sued for by the Commissioners of Health, in their name of office, unless otherwise herein provided.

§ 32. It shall be the duty of the Mayor and the Offences to Commissioners of Health, and of each of them, to be reported to Dis- give information to the District Attorney of the city trict Attorney and county of New-York, of all offences against ney the provisions of this act that shall come to their knowledge, that he may prosecute the offenders without delay, in the Court of Sessions of the city.

§ 33. No suit, that shall be brought by the Board, Suits not or Commissioners of Health, or the Health Officer, abate. or City Inspector, in their respective names of office, in pursuance of the authority given in this act, shall abate, on account of the death of the officer or officers by whom the same shall be commenced.

§ 34. The provisions of the foregoing titles of Declarato this act shall extend to all diseases which, in the ry. opinion of the Board of Health, or of the Mayor and Commissioners of Health, shall be deemed dangerous to the public health; and nothing in this act shall be construed to interfere with the remedies against nuisances, provided by the common law.

Act to be printed and distributed. § 35. The Mayor and the Commissioners of Health shall from time to time cause such parts, as they shall deem necessary of this act, to be printed, and shall deliver the same to the respective pilots of the port for distribution to the masters of vessels subject to quarantine.

Duties of magistrates. § 36. It shall be the special duty of all magistrates and civil officers, and of all citizens of the State, to aid, to the utmost of their power, the Board of Health, and all the Health Officers mentioned in this act, in the performance of their respective duties.

Bills of Health. § 37. Bills of Health to masters of vessels shall be granted by the Mayor.

Repeal. § 38. The Act entitled, "An Act concerning Quarantine, and regulations in the nature of Quarantine, at the port of New-York," passed May 13th, 1846, is hereby repealed; but such repeal shall be in no wise construed or deemed to revive any act or part of any act repealed thereby. And all other laws inconsistent with this Act are hereby repealed.

But nothing contained in this act shall be construed as repealing any part of the act entitled, "An Act to amend the Charter of the City of New-York," passed April 2d, 1849.

TITLE IV.*

OF THE MARINE HOSPITAL AND ITS FUNDS.

ARTICLE FIRST.

§ 1. The institution belonging to this State, now known as the Marine Hospital, and all the lands and buildings thereon, and all lands and buildings which may hereafter be purchased or erected and designated for such Marine Hospital, or lands and buildings used for quarantine purposes, are hereby vested in the Commissioners of Emigration, to be by them held in trust for the people of this State and the sole and exclusive control of the same, except in regard to the sanitary treatment of the in

Marine Hospital, in whom vested

---

* By the original fourth title, the Marine Hospital was placed in charge of the Commissioners of Health, and provision was made for its support by the collection of " Hospital Moneys." By chapter 483 of the laws of 1847, it was transferred to the Commissioners of Emigration, whose offices had been created by chapter 195 of the laws of that year. Since that time, various acts have been passed relative to their powers and duties. Such portions of them as do not refer to the Marine Hospital, or the Officers of Health, have been omitted in this compilation, which is intended to embrace only such laws as strictly relate to the public health.

mates thereof, is hereby given to the said Commissioners of Emigration, for the purpose of receiving therein all persons for whom bonds may be required, or for whom any bond or bonds may have been given, required, or commuted for, under the provisions of this act, or the acts hereby amended, suffering under or afflicted with any contagious or infectious disease, or other disease preventing their immediate removal to any more distant hospital, and who shall be sent to such hospital by the direction of the Health Officer or under his authority. (1847, *ch.* 483, § 1, *as amended* 1849, *ch.* 350, § 6.)

[Modified, see post section 4.]

§ 2. The Commissioners of Emigration are authorized to employ, and appoint, and dismiss at pleasure, a superintendent, physicians, and such other officers, nurses and orderlies, and such servants as they shall deem necessary for the management and care of the Marine and other hospitals

Nurses and Orderlies, &c.

used for quarantine purposes, and to pay all needful expenses therefor out of the moneys under their control ; but the moneys received under any of the provisions of this act as commutation money, or upon bonds given for or on account of any persons or passengers landing from vessels at the Port of New-York, or elsewhere, shall not be applied or appropriated to any other purpose or use than to defray the expenses incurred for the care, support or maintenance of such persons or passengers, nor shall such passengers be entitled to any aid from the Commissioners of Emigration after

they shall have left the State of New-York, and
been absent therefrom for more than one year.
Nothing in this act contained shall be deemed to
affect the authority of the Board of Health, nor the Restric-tion.
mode of appointment of the Health Officer, Resi-
dent Physician, or Commissioners of Health of the
city of New-York, or to prevent the Health Officer from selecting his own medical assistants, other
than those of the Marine Hospital, for any duties
required by law to be discharged by him, or under
his authority. (1849, *ch.* 350, § 8, *as amended* 1851,
ch. 523, § 5.)

§ 3. The Health Officer shall not by right of of- Authority
fice, have any other authority over the Marine of Health Officer.
Hospital or medical charge, as Physician thereof,
than is in this act provided. (1849, *ch.* 350, § 14.)

§ 4. There shall be nominated by the Governor, Physician
and appointed by him, with the consent of the Sen- of Marine Hospital.
ate, a Physician of Marine Hospital, whose powers
and duties shall be as follows :

1. To select and appoint, subject to the approval His duties.
of the Commissioners of Emigration, such and so
many assistant physicians, nurses, orderlies, and
other employes of the Marine Hospital as may
be found necessary for the care and management
of the said Hospital, and the proper treatment of
the inmates thereof, and to suspend or remove the
same ; but the rate of pay of the said assistant
physicians, nurses, orderlies, and other employes,

shall be regulated and determined by the Commissioners of Emigration.

2. To have the general charge and control of the Marine Hospital, and to make and enforce such rules and regulations for the government of the same, and the treatment of the sick inmates thereof as shall seem to him necessary and expedient, to maintain the said Marine Hospital as a quarantine establishment.

3. To report to the Health Officer in writing, from time to time, and as often as may be, the persons sufficiently recovered from sickness to be discharged from said hospitals, or any of them.

4. To receive into the Marine Hospitals all persons of contagious, infectious, or pestilential disease, which may be sent thither by the Health Officer, or under his authority, or under the authority of the Board of Health of the city of New-York, except itch and syphilis, which shall not be construed as diseases entitling those suffering from them to be admitted as patients into the Marine Hospital;

5. And to allow or permit the Health Officer at all times to have free access to the several wards of the Marine Hospital, for the purpose of examining the sick inmates thereof, in order to enable the said officer to judge as to the necessity for detaining the vessels from which said sick may have been

landed. (1849, *ch.* 350, § 17; *as amended* 1853, *ch.* 224, § 4, *and* 1856, *ch.* 147, § 35.)

§ 5. The Physician of Marine Hospital shall have and receive an annual salary of five thousand dollars, to be paid quarterly; and each of the assistant physicians shall have and receive a salary of one thousand two hundred dollars per annum, to be paid quarterly or monthly, as the Commissioners of Emigration may determine, and in that ratio for any period of service of such physician or assistant, and all salaries and other compensation, of such physician and assistant physicians, and of all nurses, orderlies, and servants, or others necessarily employed in and about the business, care, and proper management of such Marine or other hospital for quarantine purposes, shall be paid by the Commissioners of Emigration, from and out of moneys collected upon the bonds hereinbefore required to be given by the owners or consignees of vessels arriving with and landing passengers at the port of New-York, or from the commutation moneys paid upon or in lieu of such bonds, in accordance with the provisions of this act, and all the expenses of such marine or other hospital for quarantine purposes, shall, as far as practicable, be defrayed by said Commissioners out of and from the moneys and securities in this act specified; but nothing in this act contained shall be so construed as to authorize the payment of any salary or com-

[Margin notes:] Modified as to assistants. [See ante. § 4, sub. 1st.]

Salaries.

Restriction

pensation for services rendered by said Commissioners of Emigration, or any of them. (1849, *ch.* 350, § 20.)

Annual report of Physician of Marine Hospital.

§ 6. The Physician of Marine Hospital shall present to the Legislature, annually, on or before the first of March, a report of the general condition of the Hospital under his charge, with the statistics of the Institution in detail, and such other information and suggestions in regard to the same as he may deem advisable, and testify the same by his affidavit; he shall also furnish to the Board of Health of the city of New-York, and to the Commissioners of Emigration, whenever required by them to do so, an official return of the numbers and diseases of the patients in the Marine Hospital. (1853, *ch.* 224, § 9.)

Report of Superintendent.

§ 7. It shall be the duty of the Superintendent of the Marine or other hospital, used for quarantine purposes, to furnish to the Board of Health, as often as may be required, a full and correct report of all persons in the said hospital affected with any contagious or infectious disease, and of all such patients as may die or be discharged as cured; such report shall be countersigned by the agent of the Board of Health, and no persons who may be, or who have been received as patients affected with contagious or infectious diseases, or under treatment as such, shall be discharged or removed from the Marine or other hospital used for quarantine purposes, without a permit in writing from the Health Officer. (1849, *ch.* 350, § 12.)

§ 8. The Physician of Marine Hospital shall discharge the duties of Superintendent of Marine Hospital, under the Commissioners of Emigration, and without further pecuniary compensation than that allowed him as physician. (1853, *ch.* 224, § 12.)

Physician to be Superintendent.

§ 9. The Commissioners of Emigration shall receive into the Marine, or other hospital for quarantine purposes, all alien passengers for whom bonds shall have been given, or commutation paid, under the several acts of this State relating to alien passengers arriving at the port of New-York, who shall be affected with any contagious or infectious disease, and sent to such hospital by the authority of the Health Officer. They shall defray the expenses of such patients out of the moneys by them received on account of bonds or commutation. They shall also receive and provide for all other patients or passengers who shall have landed from any vessel at the port of New-York, affected with any contagious or infectious disorders, who shall be directed to be so received by the Health Officer, or the Board of Health; they shall be entitled to receive for each person so admitted (other than aliens above mentioned,) at the rate of three dollars per week for their support and medical care, which shall be at the expense of the owner or consignee

What alien passengers are to be received into Hospital.

of any vessel in which such person shall have arrived, and from which they have landed, and no
vessel shall be permitted to leave quarantine until
such expense shall have been paid, or secured to
be paid, to the satisfaction of the Commissioners of
Emigration, or the officer duly authorized by them
for such purpose. (1849, *ch.* 350, § 13.)

Employes
where to
reside.

§ 10. All officers and employes of the Marine
Hospital, except chaplains, shall be required to reside within the quarantine enclosure, and the Commissioners of Emigration are hereby directed to
provide suitable accommodations for the same.
(1853, *ch.* 224, § 7.)

MISCELLANEOUS PROVISIONS.

Vacancies
in Office of
Commis-
sioner of
Health,
how filled.

§ 1. The Board of Health may supply any va-
cancy that may occur in the office of either of the
Commissioners of Health of the city of New-York,
whether arising from the temporary inability of the
officer to discharge his duties, or otherwise; but
the person so appointed shall hold his office only
until such inability be removed, or the sense of the
Governor, or of the Governor and Senate, be declared. (*Part* II. *ch.* V. *Title* V. § 18, *R. S.*)

Health Of-
ficer to
take ch'ge
of effects
of persons

§ 2. Whenever any effects of a deceased person,
of which the public administrator is authorized to
take charge, shall be at the Quarantine at the
time of the death of such person, or shall arrive

there afterwards, it shall be the duty of the Health Officer, or his deputy, whichever shall be present, to secure the said effects from waste and embezzlement, and immediately give information of such effects to the public administrator, to cause an inventory, or account thereof, to be taken, and to deliver the same to the said public administrator, unless the said property be of such a description as ought not to be removed, or may be ordered to be destroyed under the laws concerning the public health. (*Part* II. *ch.* VI. *Title* VI. § 14, *R. S.*) — dying at Quarantine.

§ 3. The Health Officer shall not grant a permit to any vessel subject to quarantine, to approach the city of New-York beyond the place assigned for Quarantine, until satisfactory evidence shall be adduced, that all hospital money demanded from the master of such vessel has been duly paid, or until satisfactory security be given that the same will be paid. (1854, *ch.* 172, § 6.) — Hospital moneys to be paid before vessel proceeds.

§ 4. The Board of Health of the city of New-York may appoint any physician in their employ, or in that of the Commissioners of Emigration, to act as the agent of the Board of Health, in all matters concerning the protection of the city against the introduction of contagious or infectious diseases. (1849, *ch.* 350, § 11.) — Board of Health may appoint an agent.

§ 5. The Commissioners of Emigration may, when in their opinion it shall seem necessary, appoint a proper person or persons, to board vessels — Commissioners of Emigrat'n to appoint agents to board vessels.

from foreign ports at the Quarantine Ground or elsewhere in the port of New-York, having on board emigrant passengers, for the purpose of advising such emigrants and putting them on their guard against fraud and imposition ; and the Health Officer is hereby required to prevent any person or persons from going on board such vessels, which may be subject to examination by him, until after the said person or persons, appointed by the Commissioners of Emigration, shall have had sufficient opportunity to perform their duty, (1848, *ch.* 219, § 6.)

Trustees of Seamen's Fund and Retreat to contract for support of sick.

§ 6. It shall be the duty of the said trustees (*of the Seamen's Fund and Retreat,*) to contract with the Health Commissioners for the support of sick and disabled seamen who were subject to quarantine, and shall pay to the said Commissioners the reasonable expenses, so contracted for, of all such sick and disabled seamen during the time they shall be subject to quarantine and remain at the Marine Hospital under their direction. (1854, *ch.* 172, § 7.)

Health Officer may call on police to enforce his orders.

§ 7. The Health Officer of the Port of New-York shall have power at all times, to call upon any of the police force of the district, to a number not exceeding ten, to aid him upon any necessary emergency in enforcing the powers and duties conferred upon his office by law, and it shall thereupon become the duty of any such member of the police force, so called upon, to obey him. But such service shall not continue longer than twenty-four hours. (1857, *ch.* 569, § 19.)

An Act of Congress Respecting Quarantine and Health Laws, Passed Feb. 25, 1799.

§ 1. That the quarantines and other restraints, which shall be required and established by the health laws of any State, or pursuant thereto, respecting any vessel arriving in, or bound to, any port or district thereof, whether from a foreign port or place, or from another district of the United States, shall be duly observed by the collectors and all other officers of the revenue of the United States, appointed and employed for the several collection districts of such State respectively, and by the masters and crews of the several revenue cutters, and by the military officers who shall command in any fort or station upon the sea-coast; and all such officers of the United States shall be, and they hereby are, authorized and required, faithfully to aid in the execution of such quarantines and health laws, according to their respective powers and precincts, and as they shall be directed from time to time by the Secretary of the Treasury of the United States. And the said Secretary shall be, and he is hereby authorized, when a conformity to such quarantine and health laws shall require

Quarantine &c., by the laws of the States to be observed by officers of the United States.

To aid in their execution.

Sec'y of Treas'y may vary regulat'ns as to entr͏ and rep͏

o' vessels and cargoes. it, and in respect to vessels which shall be subject thereto, to prolong the terms limited for the entry of the same, and the report or entry of their cargoes, and to vary or dispense with any other regulation applicable to such reports and entries : *Provided,* That nothing herein shall enable any State to collect a duty of tonnage or impost without the consent of the Congress of the United States thereto ; and *provided,* That no part of the cargo of any vessel shall, in any case, be taken out or unladen therefrom, otherwise than as by law is allowed, or according to the regulations hereinafter established.

Provisos.

If prohibited from coming to ports of entry, &c., may discharge elsewhere. § 2. That when, by the health laws of any State, or by the regulations which shall be made pursuant thereto, any vessel arriving within a collection district of such State, shall be prohibited from coming to the port of entry or delivery by law established for such district, and it shall be required or permitted by such health laws, that the cargo of such vessel shall or may be unladen at some other place within or near to such district, the collector authorized therein, after due report to him of the whole of such cargo, may grant his especial warrant or permit for the unlading and discharge thereof, under the care of the surveyor, or of one or more inspectors, at some other place where such health laws shall permit, and upon the conditions and restrictions which shall be directed by the Secretary of the Treasury, or which such collector may, for the time, reasonably judge expedient for the security of the public revenues; *Provided,* That in every such case, all the articles of the cargo so to be unladen, shall be deposited at the risk of the parties concerned therein, in such public or other warehouses or inclosures as the collector shall designate, there to remain under the joint custody of such collector and of the owner or owners, or master, or other person having charge of such vessel, until the same shall be entirely unladen or discharged; and until the goods, wares or merchandize which shall be so deposited, may be safely removed without contravening such health laws; and when such removal may be allowed, the collector having charge of such goods, wares or merchandize, may grant permits to the respective owners, or consignees, their factors or agents, to receive all goods, wares or merchandize, which shall be entered, and whereof the duties accruing shall be paid or secured according to law, upon the payment by them of a reasonable rate of storage; which shall be fixed by the Secretary of the Treasury for all public warehouses and inclosures.

§ 3. That there shall be purchased or erected, under the orders of the President of the United States, suitable warehouses with wharves and inclosures, where goods and merchandize may be unladen and deposited, from any vessel which shall be subject to a quarantine, or other restraint, pursuant to the health laws of any State as aforesaid,

Warehouses procured for such cargoes.

at such convenient place or places therein, as the safety of the public revenue, and the observance of such health laws may require.

APPENDIX.

Extract from an Ordinance passed April 9th, 1839.

§ 3. It shall be the duty of the Resident Physician and Health Commissioner to attend the meetings of the Board of Health, and to communicate such information and perform such acts as may be equired of them by the said Board.

Resolution of the Board of Health, passed June 8, 1854.

Resolved, That the Commissioners of Health be requested to attend the meetings of this Board until directed to the contrary.

Resolution of the Board of Health, passed July 2, 1856.

Resolved, That the Health Officer of this Port be, and he is hereby directed to tranship on suitable lighters, all emigrant passengers arriving at this port, and to fumigate, ventilate and otherwise cleanse the vessels in which they shall arrive, whenever the condition of said passengers or vessels shall require the same to be done, for the protection of the public health.

Transhipment of Emigrant passeng'rs.

Extract from the minutes of a meeting of the Commissioners of Health, held July 1, 1857.

Old beds and bedding a nuisance in the Bay. " A letter was presented by his Honor the Mayor, from Mayor Powell of Brooklyn, in relation to the throwing overboard of refuse materials and bedding from vessels arriving in the Bay, and the following resolutions adopted:

Resolved, That the practice of throwing refuse beds, bedding, clothing, &c., from vessels into the waters of the harbor is a nuisance.

Resolved, That the Health Officer be requested to take measures to have it abated.

Provision for the iron scow. *Resolved,* That the Resident Physician (Dr. Rockwell,) be authorized to procure an Iron Scow, and the necessary outfit, to be used for the purpose of burning infected and refuse articles under the direction of the Health Officer.

The following were also adopted:

Evasion of quarantine by vessels and cargoes entering port clandestinely. *Whereas,* It has been represented to this Board, that many vessels from the West Indies carrying cargoes consigned to, or owned at this Port, for the purpose of evading our Quarantine Laws, are sent for their port of entry to some small town along our sea-board, and from thence they bring or send in smaller vessels their cargoes directly to the wharves of our city, without being subject to an examination of the Health Officer:

And whereas, The occurrence of several isolated cases of Yellow Fever, originating from vessels and cargoes thus clandestinely brought to our city during the Summer of 1856, taught this Board that to permit such infractions of the Health Laws was imminently dangerous to the public health, therefore :

Resolved, That the Health Officer be, and he is hereby requested to give immediate attention to this new and repeated attempt at evading the Quarantine Laws by removing to quarantine or to quarantine anchorage, all such foreign vessels, or vessels and cargoes, recently from the West India ports, which may arrive at our wharves, or be landed in our city within thirty days of their Custom House entry or report.

Health Officer to remove to Quarantine.

Resolved, That the Inspector of vessels be, and he is hereby directed, by inspection or otherwise, to assist in the detection of these evasions of our Health Laws, and to report to this Board all the facts in relation thereto as soon as practicable."

Inspector of vessels to aid.

Resolutions of the Commissioners of Health, passed July 13th, 1857.

Resolved, That all vessels coming from ports where Yellow Fever prevailed at the time of their

Vessels from infected ports must lighter their cargoes.

departure shall discharge their cargoes on lighters at Quarantine.

Resolved, That all vessels having had the fever on Board while in their ports of departure, or during their passage to this port, or after their arrival, shall in all cases discharge their cargoes in the lower Bay.

Resolved, That all vessels from infected ports, having had no cases of the fever amongst their crews while in their ports of departure, or on their passage to this port, or after their arrival in port, shall be permitted to discharge their cargoes on lighters at the upper quarantine anchorage.

The following Resolutions were passed by the Mayor and Commissioners of Health, May 20, 1858.

Duty of Inspector of vessels.

Resolved, That the Inspector of Vessels be, and he is hereby directed to personally inspect the cargo of every coastwise vessel, not subject to quarantine, and the cargo of every vessel which shall consist in whole or in part of fruit, cotton, wool, rags, hemp, hides, skins, bones or horns, arriving at this port between the first day of April and the first day of November.

To report daily to the Mayor.

Resolved, That the Inspector of Vessels be, and he is hereby directed to cleanse and purify such vessels, arriving at or being in the immediate vicinity of the wharves of the city, as the Mayor from time to time shall direct; and that he be and is hereby required to report to this Board daily the condition of every vessel and cargo so cleansed and inspected by him.

Resolved, That each and every resolution, and all directions hitherto passed upon by this Board, inconsistent with the foregoing resolutions, are hereby rescinded.

PORT OF NEW-YORK.

QUARANTINE GROUND.

STATEN ISLAND, 1858.

RULES AND REGULATIONS TO BE OBSERVED BY MASTERS OF VESSELS UNDER QUARANTINE.

1. Quarantine Colors must be worn in the main shrouds of all vessels at Quarantine until the commander shall be furnished with a bill of health—and a light must be hoisted at night.

2. All persons whatever, belonging to a vessel at Quarantine, are strictly prohibited from going on shore, except at the Health Office wharf, unless by permission of the Health Officer.

3. All persons whatever, belonging to a vessel at Quarantine, are forbidden to take on board with them any person who did not arrive in such vessel and all passengers or other persons who live on shore, are also prohibited from going on board their own vessels, except by permission of the Health Officer.

4. All communication between vessels put under Quarantine is expressly prohibited.

5. No boat shall be permitted to come on shore

without an officer in it, and only between sun rising and sun setting, unless in cases of distress or sickness; and all boats must be alongside or on board by sun-down. The bell of the Health Office boathouse will be rung ten minutes before sun-down, to give notice to all boats to go off to their respective vessels.

6. On Sundays, all boats must put off to their vessels by ten o'clock in the morning, when the bell will be rung to give such notice; and the boats must not come on shore again before six o'clock in the evening.

7. ☞ No boat or craft is permitted to go alongside of a vessel at Quarantine, and no person is permitted to board a vessel at Quarantine, or to have intercourse, communication or dealing with her crew or passengers, for any purpose whatever, without a written permit from the Health Officer.

Intercourse with vessels prohibited.

8. Provisions and other necessaries, intended to be sent on board of a vessel at Quarantine, must be embarked from the Health Office wharf only, except the Health Officer grants as a special permit to proceed to any other wharf.

9. No rum or spirituous liquors shall be sent or taken on board of vessels at Quarantine, except an *order* from the commander of the vessel, signed by the Health Officer.

10. Commanders of vessels are accountable for all irregularities committed on board their respective vessels, and for the conduct of such of their people as they may send on shore; and if any person shall elope from their vessel, a report thereof must be immediately made to the Health Officer.

11. Universal cleanliness must be preserved on board.

12. Wind-sails must be constantly kept up in each hatchway, and trimmed to the wind; except on account of the weather, or discharging the cargo.

13. The bilge-water must be completely pumped out at least twice a day, and water from alongside be put in the pump, until the water so pumped out shall be clear and free from any offensive smell.

14. All foul wearing apparel and bed-clothes of the steerage passengers, and all wearing apparel and bed-clothes of the officers and seamen, must be washed and aired; the beds emptied and the ticks washed, when the filling may be put in again, if it is in good condition.

No beds or refuse material to be thrown into the Bay.

15. ☞ No refuse beds or bedding or other material must be thrown overboard from any vessel under or subject to Quarantine; and the master of each and every said vessel is hereby notified to burn such refuse material immediately on arrival.

16. The forecastle and steerage to be scrubbed, scraped, and then washed throughout with a solution of CHLORIDE OF LIME.

17. All infractions of the foregoing rules will be punished as the law directs, viz:

☞ "Every master of a vessel subject to Quarantine, or visitation by the Health Officer, arriving in the port of New-York, who shall refuse or neglect, either to remain with his vessel at Quarantine during the period assigned for her Quarantine, and while at Quarantine, to comply with the directions and regulations prescribed by law, and with such as any of the Officers of Health, by virtue of the authority given to them by law, shall prescribe in relation to his vessel, his cargo, himself, his passengers, or crew, shall be guilty of a misdemeanor, and be punished by a fine not exceeding two thousand dollars, or by imprisonment not exceeding twelve months, or by both such fine and imprisonment."

R. H. THOMPSON,
Health Officer.

COMMISSIONERS OF HEALTH.

1857—8.

DANIEL F. TIEMANN, Mayor,
AND PRESIDENT COMMISSIONERS OF HEALTH.
Office, City Hall.
Residence, Manhattanville.

R. H. THOMPSON, M. D.
HEALTH OFFICER.
Office, Quarantine Grounds.
Residence, Tompkinsville, Staten Island.

WILLIAM ROCKWELL, M. D.
RESIDENT PHYSICIAN.
Office, Mayor's Office, City Hall.
Residence, No. 50 East 11th Street, New-York.

JEDEDIAH MILLER, M. D.
HEALTH COMMISSIONER.
Office, Mayor's Office, City Hall.
Residence, No. 17 Avenue D, New-York.

GEORGE W. MORTON, Esq.
CITY INSPECTOR.
Office, No. 1 Centre Street.
Residence, No. 55 Vandam Street.

JOHN CLANCY, Esq.
PRESIDENT BOARD OF ALDERMEN.
Office, No. 65 Bayard Street.
Residence, No. 85 Elm Street.

CHARLES H. HASWELL, Esq.
PRESIDENT BOARD OF COUNCILMEN.
Office, 6 Bowling Green.
Residence, 59 East 31st Street.

J. B. AULD, Esq.
CLERK TO THE COMMISSIONERS OF HEALTH.
Mayor's Office.
Residence, 215 West 42d Street.